THE M
MISSI

The mysterious disappearance of
Uncle Stanley's garden gnome caused
uproar in Gilly's family. Who took it?
Who sent the puzzling postcards?

Any number of people might have
been responsible — for different
reasons, of course. Can Gilly uncover
the culprit? Can you?

Leone Peguero's mystery will hold
you in suspense, but her witty style
will keep you laughing right to the
exciting conclusion of this book.

Editor: Rodney Martin

For Laura and Stan.

(L.P.)

Produced by Martin International Pty Ltd
[A.C.N. 008 210 642] South Australia
Published in association with Era Publications,
220 Grange Road, Flinders Park, South Australia 5025

Text © Leone Peguero, 1993
Illustrations © Amanda Graham, 1993
Printed by Hyde Park Press, South Australia
First published 1993

**National Library of Australia
Cataloguing-in-Publication Data:**

Peguero, Leone.
        The mystery of the missing garden gnome.

        ISBN 1 86374 060 0.

        1. Readers (Primary). I. Title.
        (Series : Junior novel).

428.6

Available in:

Australia from Era Publications, 220 Grange Road,
Flinders Park, South Australia 5025

Canada from Vanwell Publishing Ltd, 1 Northrup Cresc.,
PO Box 2131, Stn B, St Catharines, ONT L2M 6P5

New Zealand from Wheelers Bookclub, PO Box 35-586
Browns Bay, Auckland 10

Singapore, Malaysia & Brunei from Publishers Marketing
Services Pte Ltd, 10-C Jalan Ampas,
#07-01 Ho Seng Lee Flatted Warehouse, Singapore 1232

Southern Africa from Trade Winds Press (Pty) Ltd,
PO Box 20194, Durban North 4016 RSA

United States of America from AUSTRALIAN PRESS ™,
c/- Ed-Tex, 15235 Brand Blvd, #A107, Mission Hills CA 91345

The Mystery of the Missing Garden Gnome

Written by Leone Peguero
Illustrated by Amanda Graham

JUNIOR
NOVELS

1

First there was a gnome

MY UNCLE STANLEY wanted a garden gnome, especially one in his football club colours.

"Trust Stanley!" said my mother. "Ugly little things, they are."

"Oh, I don't know," replied my Aunt Lorna, pursing her lips as if she were about to blow an umpire's whistle. And soon afterwards she bought one as a Christmas present for Uncle Stanley. I'm sure she does things like that just to annoy my mother!

Whatever my tall, dazzling, red-headed aunt's reason, there was a whole lot she didn't know about football gnomes.

"Not black and white!" gasped Uncle Stanley, as he unwrapped it.

"The black and white ones are by far the prettiest, Stanley," replied my aunt.

"But Lorna," spluttered my poor uncle, "*my* team is black and red."

"Does it really matter? It's pretty, isn't it, Gilly dear?" said Aunt Lorna, turning to me.

What could I say? Luckily, several voices, especially my older brother Robert's (he takes his football very seriously), started to tell her that it mattered a whole lot.

"What a fuss about nothing!" declared my aunt. "Still, I'll change it over. There were some nice red and white ones."

"No, Lorna," Uncle Stanley almost shouted, "red and *black*."

It *was* Christmas, so celebrations staggered on.

The trouble really began later when Aunt Lorna found there were no red and black gnomes left. Still, she was not one to be beaten easily, so she bought a tin of red paint instead!

"I'm not a flamin' artist," gasped a shocked Uncle Stanley, when the paint was handed to him.

"Don't be silly, Stanley," she snapped. "It just needs a bit of paint here and there. You can easily change the white bits to red."

A week or two later we were at their place for a barbecue lunch. Uncle Stanley was ready to unveil his masterpiece. However, as he removed the rug that covered the newly-painted gnome, Watford, his dog, leapt into his arms, collecting the gnome on the way.

The gnome landed with a sickening thud on the paving, breaking its head clean off.

We all took a deep breath, but Aunt Lorna was as determined as ever. "Why," she proclaimed, smiling severely, "it's such a clean break it will mend easily."

The next day she headed off to the hardware store and returned with some glue that the storekeeper insisted would do the job.

So the head was returned to the sad little garden gnome.

"Sane people would hide it at the bottom of the garden with all the other elves and fairies," said my mother in disgust.

But not Aunt Lorna and Uncle Stanley. They placed it in the *middle* of their front lawn!

2

Then there was no gnome!

"WHY the *front* yard?" demanded my mother. "How embarrassing having a thing like that in public view! I don't know what Bill and Jean will think when they get back!"

Luckily Bill and Jean, the people from across the road, were on extended vacation so she couldn't draw them into the debate. Anyway, there was *much* worse to come! Aunt Lorna was knitting the gnome a cap and scarf in red and black!

"She's *not* actually going to put them on it, is she?" my mother 'whispered' one evening as we left after a tense visit.

"Please keep your voice down, Gwenda," replied my father warily as we trooped past the little gnome, its eyes winking in the dark.

But that was exactly what Aunt Lorna planned to do and Uncle Stanley was clearly delighted.

"Now you haven't seen anything like that, have you?" he asked happily.

He didn't seem to notice the sarcastic tone in my mother's voice. "No doubts about *that*, Stanley."

It was the next week that the cap and scarf were stolen. Aunt Lorna telephoned with the news. But even worse was to come. The following evening the gnome itself disappeared!

After another hysterical telephone call, we all drove to the scene of the crime. It was like calling, after a death in the family. We sat quietly around large pots of tea and coffee.

Uncle Stanley was the first to lose his cool.

"If I thought that anyone I knew was responsible . . ."

"Stanley," interrupted my mother, rising grandly to her feet, "if you want to accuse your own family of stealing, please say so."

"Only as a prank, mind you, Gwenda. Stealing wasn't . . ."

My father had to restore peace. "Look here Stanley, you'll have to look somewhere else for your gnome-napper."

Obviously Uncle Stanley believed him because the next day he reported the matter to the local police.

His report, however, was not taken as seriously as he had hoped. He had expected them to visit and actually search for clues. Instead, the officer made a few notes and said that they'd keep a look out for it.

Understandably Uncle Stanley felt that his loss was not regarded as a high priority.

"I'd jolly well hope not," snorted my mother. "Let's hope the police have more important things to do!"

No wonder my harassed uncle decided to take matters into his own hands.

3

Stanley and Watford sniff out clues

UNCLE STANLEY took to walking Watford around the local district, peering about like a sea captain with a periscope.

He had no success, however, until one day he caught a glimpse of something suspicious in a backyard. He couldn't be sure, so he hovered about waiting for a chance to edge up the driveway.

You had to feel sorry for him. The occupants not only spied him, they also rang the police and reported a prowler. Stanley soon found himself pinned against a fence by a police officer and several residents.

"Now look," he exploded, "I'm the injured party here!"

"Can't see how you make that out, mate. This is private property, this is," countered a burly male resident.

This was Uncle Stanley's moment of triumph. "Because," he trumpeted, "you've got stolen property of mine in your backyard!"

This time it was the resident's turn to be outraged.

"Look here," he thundered, "you bowl in uninvited, and now make some fool claims. You're on thin ice, you are."

Not to be shouted down when he had right on his side, Uncle Stanley

fought back. "What do you call that garden gnome you've got around the back, then?"

A light dawned in the policeman's eyes. "Oh, it's *you* is it? The one with the stolen gnome."

At this point, one of the younger family members was able to get into the conversation. "Dad, he probably means that daggy old thing that Dennis brought home from the tip."

The young officer was beginning to get a grip on things. "I happen to know that this gentleman here has been on the lookout for some property of his. Perhaps you'd be so good as to help out with our enquiries."

They all marched round to the backyard.

"That horrible little thing *stolen*! That belongs to my son, Dennis."

Uncle Stanley's face must have been something to see. The little gnome in front of him was black and red all right, but not the way his had been. This one had been painted black, but then it had had red paint dripped over it as if it were blood. It also had safety pins stuck on its ears, chains around its neck and waist, and worst of all, its little peaked hat had been broken off and a red wig stuck in its place.

It was not a pretty sight!

"It's all yours, mate," declared the shocked resident to an overcome Stanley.

"Gosh Dad, Dennis will chuck a wobbly if you give it away," said his young daughter.

There was, of course, no danger of Uncle Stanley wanting the catastrophe that stood before him, so he left it and headed off home faster than a racing driver on a spin out.

4

A few surprises

THE FAMILY GRAPEVINE was in full flourish with more gnome news.

"Guess what?" said my mother over breakfast. "The gnome's cap and scarf are back!"

"How did they get back?" asked Robert.

"Mail."

"Any postmark?" asked Dad.

"Up north."

"So it's not the people around the corner where Stanley saw the funky gnome," I concluded.

"Ah!" she replied knowingly. "Stanley is convinced that it is and that this is just a ploy to put him off."

Fascinating conversation though it was, we all had to get off to work and school. But there was more to come that evening.

"That gnome wrote a postcard to Uncle Stanley," I cried, having rushed home from Aunt Lorna's with the latest report.

"Get away!" exclaimed Dad, looking up from his newspaper.

"It *did*. Aunt Lorna showed me. It was written in weird cut-and-paste letters." I described it in full.

* Sun Sea and Surf in Queensland!

PLEASE AFFIX STAMP HERE

dEAr STAN dOnT WORRy ABOUT ME. I'M HAvINg A GReAt TIMe UP HERE SORRY i CAN'T BE with you. JUST GET ON wiTH things yOUR GARDEN GNOmE

"That's crazy," declared Robert.

"I wonder who sent it?" said my mother thoughtfully.

"The gnome did," added Robert, spooking about.

No one took any notice of Robert's nonsense. But the intrigue grew, especially when later that week there were several more postcards, all cut-and-paste.

"This has gone far enough," my mother pronounced.

But what to do? It was my turn I decided, to do the detective thing.

5

A ring of truth

THERE WAS one obvious question staring me in the face. *Is the punk gnome really Uncle Stanley's?* If so, this was undoubtedly an open and shut case — Dennis took it! After all, why should we believe he found it at the tip?

All I needed to know was whether, underneath all the paint, the punk gnome's neck was broken. That surely would be evidence enough.

"So how are you going to find out?" asked Robert, when he heard of my plans. "I wouldn't mess with that family if I were you. That Dennis is one tough dude."

I smiled mysteriously and replied, "Women's network!"

As I knocked at the door of the suspect's house, I hoped I was right.

Even Dennis was likely to have a mother! Sure enough, there she was and happy to talk to me too.

"He said he found it at the tip, dear."

"What about the scarf and hat?" She shook her head.

"And the postcards?"

"*Dennis* write a postcard?" She laughed uproariously. "You'd have to be joking!"

Somehow her comment had a ring of truth, so perhaps Dennis was innocent.

I also managed to get her to show me the gnome. It certainly was the right kind and height. I peered closely at the layers of paint for the tell-tale crack around its neck.

"Well?" she asked eagerly.

I was just about to answer when Dennis sped around the side of the house on his bike. My mouth opened, but my voice wouldn't work.

"I've got to get home now," I finally managed to say, and I took off faster than a prize homing-pigeon.

The crack was there all right, but I didn't fancy confronting Dennis with that fact!

6

Motives and clues

I NOW FELT certain that the gnome *was* Uncle Stan's. But supposing that Dennis really did find the gnome at the tip? Who had dumped it there? And did that person also send back the knitting and mail the postcards? And if so, why?

Who had the motive and the opportunity? The answer to that had to be practically anyone. Let's face it, to heaps of lame-brained people, nicking a gnome is a real hoot!

Still, surely it was reasonable to check first whether the truth lay closer to home. Unfortunately that meant examining my own family's motives.

Did Robert, for some dopey reason, think that making the gnome vanish might be a joke?

Did my mother feel it her duty to tidy up the family image by dumping the little monster,

or was Dad tired of dealing with her over it, so took the little fellow for a ride?

Was Uncle Stanley secretly angry with Aunt Lorna for getting the wrong colours?

Maybe Aunt Lorna realized that her front yard had become a joke?

Obviously to be a good detective you had to be willing to believe the worst about *everyone!*

I decided to skip the motive for the moment and concentrate on the clues. I'd take a closer look at Exhibits A (the scarf and hat) and Exhibit B (the postcards).

I'd follow the trail wherever it led!

First stop was Aunt Lorna's to see if I could get my hands on Exhibits A and B.

Once there I offered some feeble reason for wanting to borrow them, but Aunt Lorna interrupted me. "Just take them, Gilly dear," she said with resignation. "I don't think it's doing Stan any good seeing them around."

I took the cap, scarf and cards and fled.

Now that I had them, what should I look for? For one thing, if the hat and scarf had been lying about at the tip there'd be dirt on them. I held them to the light. They were clean.

What about the postcards? The cut-and-paste words were no help. However, the address had been typed with an old-fashioned typeface. There had to be heaps of old typewriters about. Even Uncle Stan had one, I remembered.

No, I told myself, it *wasn't* him.
There was no reason for him to
send postcards. At least, none that
I could imagine.

7

The scene of the crime

IT WAS TIME to examine the scene of
the crime.

What did I expect to find on
Aunt Lorna's front lawn? Footprints,
vehicle tracks, cigarette butts?

I certainly felt silly peering around. Funny thing was, I did find something — just little bits of plaster. What did they mean? That wasn't where the head had come off, was it?

As I walked on home I made a mental list of what I knew:

1. Dennis almost certainly had Uncle Stanley's gnome.
2. Dennis probably didn't write those postcards, so someone else had to be involved.
3. Dennis probably did find the gnome at the tip.
4. It was dumped by someone who had an old typewriter and was able to mail things from far away.
5. Something had happened to the gnome on the front lawn.

Was a pattern beginning to emerge? What I needed now was an event to push matters along.

8

The gathering

THE FOLLOWING SUNDAY we were due,
as usual, at Aunt Lorna's for lunch.
At this barbecue, however, there
were more than sausages cooking.

We were settling in when Dennis
screeched down the side driveway on
his bike. It was going to be just like
the movies when all of the suspects
are thrown together.

"Who do we have here?" asked
Uncle Stan warily, never having
actually met Dennis.

"What do you mean?" replied the intrepid Dennis. "I got some note telling me to turn up." He waved a piece of paper under our noses. "Something to do with the gnome I found."

Luckily for me things moved along too quickly for anyone to wonder who had sent Dennis an invitation. My plan was working! Uncle Stan almost dropped his cooking tongs.

"Ah, the lad who stole my gnome!"

"No way," growled Dennis, taking in the parade of suspects for himself. "But I know who did." Then he pointed his finger with the authority of one who has his facts well in hand. "That's who it was!"

We all focused in the direction of his accusing finger.

9

The villain revealed!

HE WAS POINTING at Aunt Lorna!

She turned pale, knocked over a row of beer glasses and burst into tears.

We all seemed to be frozen in the moment. Then at last my mother hurried to soothe Aunt Lorna. I tried to pick up the glasses, while Watford began to lick up the spilt beer.

Stan remained motionless, until something snapped.

"Good heavens, Lorna," he said with dignity. "It's only a little garden gnome. What's all this fuss about nothing?"

"I'm sorry, Stanley. It was all my fault." Aunt Lorna sobbed. "I barely touched the silly gnome one morning and its head fell off again onto the lawn." My aunt waved her hands pantomiming the sorry event. "I just couldn't glue it together again, no matter how hard I tried. In fact," she declared snappily, "I'm sure there was something wrong with that glue. It made the plaster all crumbly and it fell all over the lawn!"

This was more like the determined Aunt Lorna we knew!

"Stanley, I just couldn't bear the idea of you seeing it like that, so I heaved it into my car and I drove it to the tip."

"I saw you drop it off," growled Dennis. "And that means it was public property."

"But Aunt Lorna, the cap and the scarf went first," said my brother Robert, surprisingly alert.

"I know. They really were stolen for a day. Someone must have had a bit of fun with us. They were sitting on the mailbox next morning. I was putting them back on, when the head came off."

"But mailing them," said my scandalized mother. "And those postcards . . ."

"The typing on the cards," I put in eagerly. "That was Uncle Stan's old typewriter, wasn't it?"

"Yes," sighed Aunt Lorna. "I thought it might help Stanley get over losing the gnome."

"But they were mailed from miles away," Dad interjected.

"No doubt by Bill and Jean, while on vacation," I supplied.

"Clever Gilly," gasped Aunt Lorna.

Then she looked as though she was about to lapse into tears again. "I'm just relieved it's all out in the open. I'll get you a new one, just as soon . . ."

"No need for that," said Uncle Stanley, as if garden gnomes had never caused him a moment's concern. "At least the mystery's been solved."

It had been a tense time, but the truth was now out and things soon lightened up, especially when we realized that Watford had been happily guzzling the spilt beer. The poor old thing was pretty shaky on his legs for the rest of the afternoon!

Dennis even offered to return the gnome, but Uncle Stanley seemed to have been cured of his obsession and offered him lunch instead.

So the mystery of the missing gnome had been solved, and we could all relax — at least until the next family drama!